Ghosts of the Carolinas

Other University of South Carolina Press Books by Nancy Roberts

The Haunted South
Where Ghosts Still Roam

South Carolina Ghosts
From the Coast to the Mountains

Ghosts of the Southern Mountains and Appalachia

The Gold Seekers
Gold, Ghosts and Legends from Carolina to California

North Carolina Ghosts & Legends

Civil War Ghost Stories & Legends

Ghosts
of the Carolinas

Nancy Roberts

Foreword by Legette Blythe

University of South Carolina Press

Copyright © 1962, 1967 by Nancy Roberts

Published in Columbia, South Carolina,
by the University of South Carolina Press

First published by McNally and Loftin,
Publishers, Charlotte, N.C. 1962

Photographs by Bruce Roberts

00 99 98   12 11 10 9 8

ISBN 0–87249–586–8 (cloth)
ISBN 0–87249–587–6 (paper)

Contents

Foreword

MILLIONS OF WORDS have been spoken and written—and effectively—in heralding the attractions and advantages of the Carolinas.

Most of this material has emphasized the physical assets of the region. Some of it has even listed the high spirits of Carolinians as important intangibles in the enumeration of assets.

These promoters of the Carolinas have given little appreciation, as far as I have observed, however, to the virtues of the most intangible of these intangibles, the spirits themselves.

Yet surely no section of the nation can rightfully claim more mystifying, more intriguing, more sadly accusing, more altruistic, or more enduring ghosts. Of a certainty we have our share of the finest shades in all America. And they have gone too long uncatalogued and unappreciated.

But this failure of our generally alert and enterprising public relations folk to exploit adequately the Carolinas' apparitions has been remedied in part at least by Nancy Roberts and her photographer husband Bruce. With the publication a few years ago of *An Illustrated Guide to Ghosts and Mysterious Occurrences in the Old North State* and now this volume on other ghosts of both Carolinas, Nancy and Bruce Roberts promulgate our claim to possession of some of the most frightening and charming and authenticated ghosts that have ever walked—or drifted or floated, or, tritely, haunted—the American scene.

The new book evenly shares between the two states certain of the more notable apparitions. Many of these shades even yet materialize, or seem to, from out of the deep past; they are venerable and respected and long have been spoken of even with affection. One such is the Gray Man of Pawley's Island, South Carolina, a benevolent ancient-young man whose appearance to those who see his apparition strolling along the beach has become a warning to flee from a closely approaching hurricane. Some are peculiarly and identifiably Carolinian; others are reported to materialize from time to time in widely separated states. Some are not even human emanations, like the ghostly Hound of Goshen, a frightening apparition that has scared the daylights out of many persons through long years. But to give that old spirit dog his due, though he has chased dozens, maybe scores or hundreds of horses, mules and terrified people to near exhaustion, he has not to this day bitten man or beast.

Difficult to classify are some of the others in this book—the Brown Mountain lights, for example. Are they the spectral torches of Indian braves slain in a long-ago battle along the mountain's ridges? Or could they be the luminous apparitions of Indian maidens seeking lovers lost in that battle? Or indeed, are they but a natural phenomenon never satisfactorily explained? There are those who think that— persons who, perish the thought, have neither eyes to see a ghost materialize nor ears to hear his almost soundless coming, nor skin sensitized to notice the sudden swift clamminess of his passing. But for a fact the lights do appear above Brown Mountain, whether ghostly, gaseous, reflected, or mirage. I have seen them myself.

To illustrate his wife's intriguing stories, Bruce Roberts has artfully planned and skillfully executed photographs of the sites of certain mysterious occurrences. And even though they may not convince all the book's readers of the reality of its spectral characters, most surely they must earn the plaudits of the more vainglorious in his ghostly gallery.

—LEGETTE BLYTHE

Huntersville, North Carolina
September, 1962

Ghosts of the Carolinas

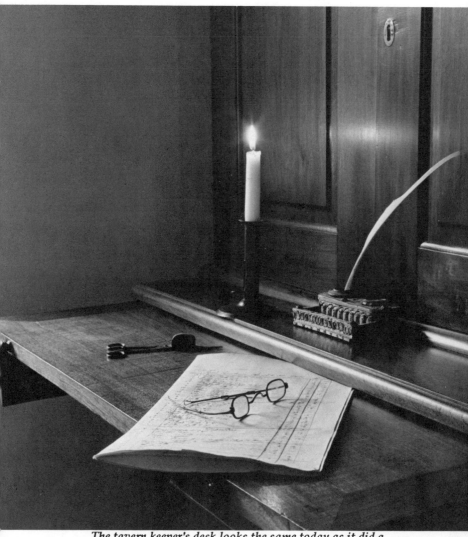

The tavern keeper's desk looks the same today as it did a hundred years ago. The Tavern is part of the Old Salem restoration at Winston-Salem.

The Talking Corpse

THE KEEPER OF OLD SALEM TAVERN NEVER FORGOT
THE NIGHT A DEAD MAN BROUGHT HIM A MESSAGE

As the keeper of Salem Tavern busily greeted new arrivals, he had not the slightest premonition that this night was to be the start of a most unusual chain of events.

It was a bitterly cold November evening and a drizzling rain added to the discomfort of travelers. Many decided to stop early and enjoy the Tavern's cheer. It was a house of entertainment with a widespread reputation for hospitality and had often been host to distinguished visitors. George Washington himself lodged here for two days on his 1791 visit to North Carolina.

As the hour grew late the social rooms emptied, the guests retired, and the tavern keeper sat alone before his upright walnut desk. His office door opened off one side of the rear of the large tavern hall. Behind it was the sitting room used by his own family. At the left of his desk was a small window which admitted enough light to allow him to see his accounts. And at the far end of the tiny cubicle stood a tall wardrobe.

Oftentimes before he went to bed the tavern keeper would check his menu for the following day. As his eyes scanned the listing of mutton, venison, vegetables, kraut, cheese, and gingerbread, he thought he heard a faint rapping sound. He stepped out into the hall and listened. There was someone at the front door.

While he threw back the heavy bolt the hall clock chimed half after eleven. He opened the door and a man staggered across the threshold. A wave of irritation swept over the tavern keeper at the thought of having to deal with a drunken traveler at this hour—and then he saw his guest's face. It was gray and drawn with suffering.

This was no drunk. It was a desperately ill man.

The tavern keeper summoned the hostler to care for his visitor's mare, seated the man in a chair in the gentlemen's room and went to arouse his two slaves. One he sent after a doctor "with all possible haste," and the other he directed to help the sick man to his room. The man was in such anguish that he could not even tell the tavern keeper his name. So the keeper decided to wait until morning to register him. By now the doctor had arrived. He examined the patient, administered some medicine from his bag and then drew the tavern keeper to one side.

"This man is gravely ill. If he is not much improved by morning, you must call me."

Shortly afterwards the patient lapsed into a coma and before morning he was dead.

Unfortunately his clothes were not marked nor did the contents of his saddlebags reveal a single clue to his identity.

After a decent burial ceremony the Parish Graveyard received his remains and the saddlebags were placed in the office wardrobe on the bare chance that they might some day be claimed.

Several days later the innkeeper's servants began to mutter uneasily. The slaves and the hostler talked of strange goings-on in the shadowy corridors of the

The hall of the old Salem tavern

tavern. They were reluctant to go through the basement alone. The hostler was as jumpy as the young maid. Nervously they claimed that "something" was haunting the place.

The tavern keeper at first laughed; then he grew increasingly exasperated as he tried without success to allay the fears of his staff. Nothing he could say seemed to calm them or discourage the apprehensive glances they cast over their shoulders as they went about their work. One night one of the slaves dropped a heavy tray which he was taking to the dining room. Afterwards he swore something had followed him into the hall.

Finally, one night, while the tavern keeper was in his office struggling over his accounts, a young maid burst in upon him, pale with fright.

Something awful is out in that hall!" she declared hysterically.

Overcome by annoyance, the tavern keeper left the maid trembling in his office and strode out into the corridor. At first it appeared to be empty. Then to his utter amazement he heard a scraping sound and a shadowy, faceless form appeared before him.

He managed to conquer his impulse to flee and heard a voice speak to him. In hollow tones the voice begged him to notify "my brother of my death." It gave the dead traveler's name and the name of a brother in Texas. Then the hall was again empty.

When he returned to his desk the tavern keeper's hands were shaking but he grasped his pen the more firmly and began a letter to the address in Texas which the voice had given him. He described his guest and went into detail about his illness and death.

It was not long before he received an answer. The reply confirmed his guest's identity and asked that the saddlebags be forwarded to the Texas home.

The instructions of the spirit were no sooner carried out than the peculiar manifestations ceased, nor did the servants ever complain again about the tavern being haunted.

The ghost had departed as soon as his errand was accomplished. But for the rest of his life the keeper of Salem Tavern told this story of "the talking corpse" and steadfastly vouched for its truth.

The Hound of Goshen

THE SHADOWS OF THE OLD STAGECOACH ROAD WERE FRIGHTENING,
INDEED, FOR TRAVELERS PURSUED BY THE GHOSTLY WHITE DOG

The ghost that pursues travelers as they pass over
the old Buncombe Road through Goshen has staked
out a five-mile stretch of the road as his own.

He has struck terror into the heart of many a
traveler between Ebenezer Church in Maybinton
township, Newberry County, and Goshen Hill in
South Carolina's Union County. After dark is his
time to roam and he has never been known to stray
from his accustomed path.

It was in 1855 that Dr. George Douglass lived in a
white-columned mansion on a high bluff overlook-
ing the stagecoach route from Charleston to
Asheville. The road below the bluff was narrow, its
banks on either side of the deep cut high and thickly
forested. The sun seldom penetrated the road's
dense shade. Often travel along it was slow because
of mud or fallen limbs and to proceed with any speed
it was necessary to go by horse.

On a late October night a slave of William Hardy in
Maybinton got sick. Hardy sent a young slave boy by
mule to fetch Dr. Douglass from Goshen Hill four
miles away, saying "Ride fast but don't overheat
him."

Dr. and Mrs. Douglass were awakened by a series
of terrified screams. The trembling boy fell in their

door, crying, "Keep dat varmint from gittin' me."

Dr. Douglass closed the hall door and lit the lamp. The boy was almost incoherent with fear.

"Marse Doc, I is so scart dat I would hab died if'n I hadn't got to yo' doah when I did. Marse Billy sarnt me here tuh fetch you to see Sam, 'cause he is awful ailin'."

"Is Sam dying?" asked the doctor.

"No suh, Sam ain't dyin'. Leas' he wa'nt when I lef'."

"Well, why are you so scared?" questioned Douglass.

"Marse Billy 'low when I lef', ride fas' but don't you let my mule git broke out in no big sweat. I wuz ridin' along jus' as moderate as I could 'til I got to de white folks' Ebenezer Church.

"Hit was there I heered somethin' and, Marse, I looked back of me and seed de awfullest varmint I eber seed in my life, an' Lawd! I hope I ain't gwine neber see such a thing agin' as long as I lib."

"What foolish thing did you see?" inquired the doctor in some exasperation.

"Marse, it wasn't nothin foolish. When I heered dat noise, I looked around and I seed de terrublist, whitest, biggest dog I is eber heered of in my life. I stuck my heels in dat ole mule and he bruk out in de fastes' run. I thought we wuz leavin' dat dog when all at onct it got in front of de mule. Dat mule reared up and I jus' did miss fallin' offen him. When I looked agin hit was stretchin' hit's eyes at me. All de time me an' dat mule was jus' shakin' an' runnin'!"

"Where do you think the dog came from?" asked the doctor.

"Hit muster come out of de ole Evans graveyard down by de chu'ch, Marster."

"How far did it follow you?"

"Dat thing neber lef' us til I started hollerin' an' driv inter yo' lane.

"You say that your master wants me to come and see Sam?"

"Yes, suh, Marse George."

"You go back home and tell you master that I will be there at daylight."

The Negro boy fell to the floor in a frenzy of fear. "Lord God, Marse George!" he pleaded. "I can't go down dat road no mo' til day!"

Dr. Douglass went out into the yard to look at the mule. He saw that the animal was wringing wet with sweat and still trembling. The doctor called one of his own servants and had him take the mule to the barn and then take the distraught young Negro in for the night.

Early next day Dr. Douglass and the slave rode to the Hardy plantation. Along the way the boy excitedly pointed out different spots where "dat dog come out las' night."

Many times since then this strange apparition has been seen in Goshen. It still causes much alarm and a number of respected and wholly reliable witnesses have seen it.

Dr. Jim Coefield saw it and was never able to account for it. He had an affectionate dog which often followed him but after they encountered the "ghost dog" his own would leave the road at a certain spot and go through the woods until the doctor had passed the trail of the ghost. Then he would rejoin his master and trot along beside him.

Berry Sanders, a Negro boy of about seventeen, saw the ghost dog one night in April of 1936. Berry worked for a Mr. Watt Henderson and every Saturday night he had to go through Goshen on his way home. On the night of April 18 when he was going through the side gate at "The Oaks" he heard a noise. Glancing back he saw the vicious looking apparition trotting after him. It was the "Hound of Goshen."

Berry's home was a mile distant and he ran every foot of the way. The neighbors heard his screams. When the boy reached the safety of his home, the dog turned back and vanished into the woods.

There are many varying accounts. The ghost dog may leap through a closed iron gate and disappear or it may spring out from a thicket along the old road. Horses and mules along this road often behave as if they are badly frightened, much to the bewilderment of their drivers. For it is not unusual for animals with their acute senses to be first aware of the hound's peculiar presence.

And if you should decide on a pleasant evening to take a horseback ride along the old road, and your steed rears back violently, or the hair along your dog's back rises, you will do well to beware the "Hound of Goshen."

For he is there.

The Ring

DEATH BRINGS A COVETED RING—AND DISASTER—TO A
GREEDY YOUNG WOMAN

Mary was the proud, petulant one of the two sisters, while Kate was gentle hearted and kind. Orphaned during their teens the girls lived in a small cottage from which could be heard the roar of the surf when the wind was high.

The men of Dare County along the Outer Banks of North Carolina first begin to test their mettle against the honing of the sea while they are still boys. And young David Blount was one of the bravest of this "bred to the sea" breed. No night was too wild or treacherous waters too turbulent for his rescue boat when the call came to bring in terrified passengers from a wrecked ship.

David courted Kate with the same fierceness of purpose that made him thrust his eager young face into the driving rain over the stormy Atlantic. At first Mary tried to divert his attentions from her meek younger sister to herself. And when that failed she took an intense dislike to him. David knew it and cared not a whit.

After a short time Kate agreed to marry him and David produced a diamond ring of surpassing beauty which he placed upon her finger. When the winds battered the little cottage at night and the sound of the sea rose in a crashing crescendo, Kate

Wreck of a wooden sailing vessel at dawn on Hatteras Island

would look at the flashing ring and say, "The fire from this ring somehow warms my spirit and I know he'll come home to me again."

But one night the sea was the victor. Savage waves assaulted the cape and the tiny, stormtossed boat

which David rode like a young Viking was struck a shattering blow. The mountainous waves crushed it as if it were a child's toy.

When they came to tell her, Kate said nothing. From then on she went silently about her tasks at home and in the village. She rarely spoke, never smiled, until as a neighbor woman said, "The girl is like a flower which the frost has touched."

As Kate became more and more remote Mary's vivaciousness seemed to increase. There was an almost expectant air about her. Occasionally someone would see Kate looking at her ring and only then did she resemble her former self for her face would take on a strange glow.

One morning the wife of a fisherman who lived nearby heard a pounding at her door and Mary's voice crying out, "Help me! Help me! Kate is dead."

That night Mary refused to let anyone keep her company as she sat with the body. Her grief seemed too great to share. A small candle burned near the head of the coffin and Mary sat at its side. For several hours she barely moved. Then she leaned forward and looked over the side of the wooden box. Her body swayed backward slightly as if hesitating, then leaned forward poised over the casket. This time her hand crept over the edge. She grasped something, tugged, gasped slightly then tugged again, every muscle tensed.

Successful, she sank back into her chair with a sigh of deep satisfaction. A moment later she rose and held her hand up to the light of the candle. On her finger glowed the diamond.

At the funeral the sobs of Kate's sister were pathetic to hear, and as she raised her hands dramatically and wrung them in her sorrow the magnificent diamond showed off to advantage.

Several nights later Mary sat alone in the cottage. The night was a wicked one and wind and sea played an eerie duet. Then came a calling at the door above the sound of the weather, "Mary, I'm so cold. Oh, Mary, please let me come in." This happened night after night until Mary could stand it no longer. Finally, she sought the advice of a neighbor woman who suggested she ask her visitor to come in and warm herself.

That night when she heard the same pleading voice at the door, she called out to it to come in. The wind blew the door open with a clatter and a shadowy form drifted through it coming to rest quite close to where Mary stood.

"Why, Kate," said Mary. "Where are your beautiful white hands?"

"In the grave, so-o cold. Oh, Mary, what have you done to me to leave me so cold in the grave?"

"Well, Kate, where is your beautiful diamond ring?"

With that the specter seized Mary's hand.

It was mid-morning when the fisherman's wife could conceal her curiosity no longer. She came over to find out how her advice had fared.

She knocked, then she called but there was no answer. Opening the unbarred door she found Mary sitting in front of the dead embers of the fire. She answered not one of the woman's stream of questions. She simply sat looking at her left hand. The fourth finger was badly bruised; the diamond ring was gone. Nor was she ever seen wearing it again.

The earliest account of the Phantom Rider of Bush River appears in a copy of *The Rising Sun* dated April 25, 1860. Published just a year before the War Between the States, it is one of the few Carolina ghost stories to have been in written form for more than a century.

The Phantom Rider of Bush River

HER LOVER KEPT HIS PROMISE TO RETURN, THOUGH NOT THE WAY SHE HAD LONGED THAT HE WOULD

In a modest log house near Bobo's Mills on the Bush River lived a Quaker father with his lovely young daughter named Charity and a stalwart son. Although South Carolina was going through the turbulence of the Revolutionary War, the life which Charity and her family shared was a quiet one.

Its tranquillity was rippled only by the occasional, carefully concealed visits of brave young Henry Galbreath. He lost no opportunity to visit Charity when scouting trips for his country brought him nearby. He came at the risk of his life for there were many Tories about who would have given much to catch him.

One dark summer night when flecks of clouds swam over the face of the moon, young Galbreath came to visit Charity. He had come to tell her "good-by" for he had enlisted in the Continental Army.

"But one year from this day, my dear, I shall be back whether dead or alive. My horse and I will come galloping up the river road, so wait for me, my lovely lass." And Charity promised. It was July of 1780 when young Henry Galbreath left to join the American Army with which General Horatio Gates was marching south to defeat Cornwallis. Unfortunately for Henry, the Continental Commander was to be defeated at Camden and both the Carolinas plunged into a night of darkness for the American cause in the South.

After the defeat at Camden, it is not clear whether young Henry, for a time, joined the small band of guerrilla fighters led by the "Swamp Fox" Francis Marion. Marion's men represented about the only organized resistance left in South Carolina for the moment against the British. General Nathanael Greene, who had been sent south by Washington to rebuild the American Army at Charlotte was reassembling his forces.

In January of 1781 the tide of the battle began to turn. Henry, who was familiar with the frontier Piedmont, became a scout for William Washington's cavalry. His knowledge of the red clay country of the Catawba and the French Broad River Valley became invaluable. As both the British and the American armies moved across the Carolinas a tall, blue robed rider moved with them. Galbreath not only knew the country, but he had come to know the enemy and wherever he went his reputation for courage accompanied him.

When the major engagement with the British came at Cowpens, it was on ground which General Morgan had carefully selected because of the advantage it gave to the Americans. The Cowpens area was a fairly open pasture where for many years traders had assembled cattle on their way to market. Thus, the rather unglamorous name for what was to become one of the great American victories of the war. Henry had ridden through this area many times down the Old Mill Gap Road and north to the ford at Broad River.

Morgan's men formed their line of battle according to plan. First the sharpshooters, then the militia and behind the militia the main line of Continentals and Virginians. William Washington's cavalry was to rally and protect the militia if the necessity arose. While the ragged Continentals waited, the British line emerged from the forest at the far end of the meadow. There were foot-soldiers in scarlet and white, kilted Highlanders and horsemen in bright hues of green and scarlet with plumed brass helmets.

The battle was a fierce one but before the hour had passed the British began to fall back.

A bitterly disappointed Tarleton accompanied by several of his officers prepared to flee. As they left the field of the disaster, one of the officers turned and fired a shot at a pursuing member of Washington's cavalry. The shot lodged in the heart of Henry Galbreath.

At the little frontier cabin on the Bush River, Charity still waited unaware of her sweetheart's death. In cheerful repetition of household chores, sewing in the afternoon under the trees and loving preparation of meals for her father and brother, the year passed.

On the day appointed for Henry's return, Charity walked often to the door of the little cabin.

Shielding her eyes from the sun, she gazed hopefully down the river road. In the afternoon, she sat beside the river and tried to lose herself in watching it shimmer past in the sunlight.

But within she was waiting . . . waiting for the galloping sound of a horse's hoofs, and for the first time in her life the familiar, silently flowing river seemed an alien presence.

That night she let her hair down about her neck and went to bed—but not to sleep. About two o'clock she heard a peculiar sound as if the wind were rising and in the distance a rhythmic galloping which grew louder until she heard it stop outside the house.

When Charity opened the door, there was a flash of light. She saw a rider astride a handsome steed. Proudly he sat his mount and from his shoulders there flowed a blue-black robe. The flash of light came twice again. Then off sped horse and rider disappearing down the river road.

The next day Charity and her father looked all about the house and road. There were no tracks on the ground nor traces to show that any living thing had been there. She knew then that Henry had returned as he had promised—but not alive.

Henry Galbreath had joined his country's forces during a period of defeat. A year later in July, when he appeared as a ghost, the battles of Guilford Courthouse and Holbrooks Hill had already been fought and the American cause saved in the Carolinas. After Galbreath's death, the British were never quite able to win another victory in the South. Cornwallis retreated into Virginia where he surrendered in October.

In later years on moonless nights, the sound of hoofbeats was often heard beginning at the battlefield of Cowpens and continuing up the road toward the little log house on the Bush River.

Galbreath's ghost or the Phantom Rider as it is most often called, became a harbinger of defeat for the British as they never again won a significant battle in the South.

The Witch Cat

TIM FARROW MET A FRIGHTFUL DEATH BECAUSE HE FAILED TO RECOGNIZE A WITCH IN THE FORM OF A BEAUTIFUL WOMAN

In the stormy and uncertain days just before the Revolutionary War a miller and his small daughter lived near Edenton, North Carolina. To Tim Farrow the British occupation of Boston and talk of the king's oppression seemed remote, indeed, from daily tasks.

His Brownrigg Mill sat beside a long earthen dam with tall cypress trees on either side. The pond was one of the largest in that vicinity. There has always been talk—to which Tim paid little heed—that its dark amber waters were bottomless.

The day's work done, the miller would fish for a while along the bank and meditate as the last rays of the sun sifted through the cypress trees. One evening at dusk he saw a figure in a small boat approaching him from the far edge of the pond. He had never ventured to the opposite bank for the dark woods which fringed it contained for him elements of mystery and dread.

At first the shadows on the water were so deep that he could not tell whether the figure in the boat was a man or woman. But much to his astonishment when the boat reached him a woman raised her arm and pushed back her bonnet to reveal the loveliest face he had ever seen.

"My journey to these parts has been a long one. And on the way my husband died," said the young woman. "Can you tell me if there is a place close by where I might lodge for the night?"

Tim Farrow's heart went out to her. It had not been long since the death of his own wife, and this lovely creature seemed so pathetically alone and helpless.

"My small daughter and I live in yonder cottage by the mill," replied Tim. "You are welcome to share what little we have."

The young woman smiled at him gratefully and he marveled at the redness of the lips curving over her small white teeth. She gathered her full black cape around her with one hand and placed the other in his as he helped her from her boat.

That night for the first time in months Tim Farrow sat down to a delicious supper and the delights of feminine companionship. Faye, as his guest called herself, was not only a fine cook but utterly beguiling. Her hair had the sheen of black satin and while he talked her large amber colored eyes fixed themselves upon him in a manner which made him feel that surely he was a most entertaining fellow. The crude, good natured miller had never met such a woman before. Why, he felt as if he could grind corn all day and come home lighthearted as a king.

Faye stayed on, with one day following another in this happy fashion. And when the first traveling minister passed their way the two were married. The miller's only care now was the aversion which his small daughter showed for the newcomer. Occasionally Faye would try to touch the child only to have her cringe and draw away. Then sparks of yellow fire would glint in the wife's beautiful eyes.

Tim began to think that his neighbors were jealous of his good fortune. It had seemed to start while he was away on a hunting trip. Faye had spent the night with a neighbor. And afterwards the woman told that she had found her big feather bed with only a little round spot mashed down in the middle just as if a cat had slept there. After that some began to make no secret of the fact that they believed Tim's wife to be a witch.

Troubles piled up for Tim. Along with the gossip, his business at the mill began to dwindle. At the same time he sensed that his young wife was tiring of him. Often he would come home in the afternoon from the mill to find her curled up asleep in her bed. He would fix their supper and generally after the meal she became more animated and vivacious.

Unfortunately, the slacking off of Tim's business was accompanied by a series of mishaps to the mill itself. He would begin to grind the grain only to find the grinding wheels jerking, jumping and sending off blue sparks. Then he would discover that nails had been placed in the grain hoppers. Sometimes when he opened the mill door in the morning Tim found sacks of corn slashed open and grain scattered all over the floor.

The angry miller could only believe that his neighbors were tormenting him. And he decided to catch whoever was playing these cruel tricks. One night instead of walking over to the country store as was sometimes his habit, he left the path to the store and went back to his mill. Letting himself in quietly, Tim hid behind the grain bags to wait for the mischief makers.

He had not been crouched there long before he heard the wind rise outside and the rumble of thunder. Soon a heavy downpour of rain beat upon the wood shingled roof and wind whistled through the crevices of the old mill. In the shattering crashes of thunder the mill quaked as if all the wheels were grinding and trembling at once. The brawny miller was not easily frightened, but the storm was so violent that he began to feel uneasy.

In a little while it spent itself but as it did a deafening din of frog voices rose from the pond. And he could not help remembering that the hoarse voiced creatures were said to be in league with the devil.

When an owl screeched eerily from somewhere in the swamp's depths Tim Farrow could feel his flesh tingle with real fear. A sense of dread engulfed him.

At that moment there came a sharp, staccato pounding on the door—as if a dozen broomsticks were rapping against it. Tim sprang from behind the sacks and seized an ax which he had placed beside him in the event of trouble. There was a brief moment of silence. Then the door of the mill flew open. In rushed a horde of tremendous cats. Backs humped and teeth bared, the cats began to inscribe menacing circles around him. As they passed they struck viciously at him with their outstretched paws.

The terrified miller soon saw that if he did not defend himself he would be clawed to death. Grasping his ax with both hands he swung mightily at a ferocious cat springing straight at him. The face with its flashing yellow eyes was close upon him as his ax swept through the air and landed on the animal's right paw, completely severing it. The cat gave one terrible cry of pain and with ear-piercing screams and caterwauling the whole band fled out the door through which they had come.

Bleeding from the scratches the cats had inflicted, Tim stumbled out of the mill and back to his cottage. He found his wife in their bedroom. She lay on the bed in a rapidly widening pool of blood. To his horror he saw that it flowed from her right arm.

The arm had been neatly severed at the wrist.

Before the wretched man could speak his wife leaped out of the bed and her body took on the shape of a monstrous cat. Eyes blazing, it streaked past him out of the house.

As he stood like a man in a nightmare, struggling to recover himself, he heard the menacing sound of rushing water. He knew he must get to the dam gate before the roaring freshet reached it. Tim Farrow ran with frantic speed along the dam to raise the gate and save the mill. But he was too late. As he ran the dam began to tremble beneath him. The trees at the edge tottered crazily. Then the earth gave way.

With a terrified scream the miller lost his footing and toppled into the rushing black flood. As he went under his arms thrashed the water and his hands sought desperately for something to cling to.

In a few seconds more than a hundred feet of the mill dam had been swept away. Some said the bottomless depths of the pond claimed Tim Farrow's body forever. But another tale was told when the lights were low and the children safely asleep.

'Twas said then that a lone fisherman found the body floating near the darkly forested shore opposite the dam . . . And one tightly clenched hand held fast to the cleanly severed paw of a cat!

The Gray Man

HIS APPEARANCE MEANS DANGER IS NEAR, AND THOSE WHO SEE HIM DO WELL TO HEED HIS WARNING

He has strolled the strand at Pawley's Island since 1822. And when the Gray Man walks, danger is close at hand. For it has long been the practice of this benign apparition to show himself as a warning of impending disaster. His presence was again reported just before the Tidal Wave of 1893 near the old house now owned by the F. W. Lachicottes. And he is most likely to show himself in late September or October during the hurricane season.

The legend of the Gray Man was revived in April 1954. A prominent South Carolina woman who had been coming to Pawley's for twenty years brought her children and grandchildren that month for a visit.

Arriving late on a Thursday afternoon, the entire family went to look at the ocean. The grandmother was standing on the raised walkway that led from her home to the top of the dunes. As she looked toward the beach she saw a man of medium build walking northward along the water's edge. He was dressed in gray from head to toe, and he strode along swinging his arms. She watched the man look up at the dunes where she stood and thought at first that he must belong to her party.

Then he became less and less distinct. In her amazement she called out to her family, "Look at that man. He's disappearing!" In a moment what had been a man became a grayish blur. Then even that was gone. Where he had stood there was nothing. He had disappeared before the others realized he was there.

The following day was a miserable one. Vicious winds lashed at the little island and for twenty-four hours weather bulletins predicted possible tornado damage along the coast.

There are numerous Gray Man stories. A recent graphic account comes from a young Georgetown automobile dealer named Bill Collins. His family has owned a home on the Island since he was born.

This pleasant, down-to-earth young man had treated the story of the Gray Man with amused skepticism all his life. He does so no longer.

Just before hurricane Hazel struck, Collins and his wife were staying at the island while he waited to go into military service.

"Just before dusk," Collins says, "I went down to our lookout, a small wooden deck which was perched on top of the dunes and connected by a boardwalk to our house. As I stood there I saw someone walking along the beach. I was curious because there are so few people on the island in October.

"When the person coming toward me got in close focus he simply vanished. I went down to the beach and searched, but there was no sign of a living soul.

What puzzled me was the fact that because of the high dunes there was no way for anyone to get off the beach without my seeing him. My wife was amazed when I went back and told her about it.

"About a week later we were all awakened one morning at five o'clock by a loud, insistent pounding on the front door. When I opened it an elderly man stood there dressed in old clothes. He told me the Red Cross had asked him to warn everyone to leave the island. Within an hour we were gone. But the funny part of it is that I had never seen the old fellow before nor have I ever seen him again.

"I asked some of our friends about him and no one seemed to know what I was talking about. They had never seen him. Pawley's is just like a small town where everybody knows everybody else, if not by name at least by sight. But I've never been able to find

anyone who was warned by or even saw this old man.

"Soon after we left the island, Hazel hit. When we returned after the storm our lookout was gone. Houses had been washed away within a block of us and dunes 30 feet high had disappeared. We could hardly believe it when we found our own house untouched. The TV antenna hadn't even blown down. Beach towels my wife had left hanging on the porch to dry were still right where she had left them. That's part of the Gray Man legend—that no harm comes to those who see him."

"I've been ribbed a lot about this story, you know," adds Collins, smiling wryly, "but it actually happened just the way I've told it."

Who is the Gray Man and why does he walk the beach at Pawley's Island before a storm? There are many stories of his origin. The first originated, we are told, in 1822 before the calamitous storm which cost so many lives.

At this time North Inlet below Pawley's Island was a popular resort with the population of a small town. Many plantation owners had summer homes here. The pretty daughter of one of them was spending the summer with her father and sisters when she received word that her fiancé, who had been abroad for two years, would soon be home.

The young man would stop to pay his respects to his own family at their house on Pawley's Island first and the ride on to North Inlet. The happy girl directed the servants to prepare his favorite dishes for a welcoming dinner and the house was adorned with flowers and greenery.

Meantime, her suitor and his Negro servant were galloping along the Pawley's Island strand. The young man was in high spirits and gaily challenged his companion to a race. Near Middleton Pond he saw a short cut through a marshy area and decided to take it. But his horse stumbled and he pitched headlong into the mire.

When he tried to get to his feet he found himself only sinking deeper into the mud. In a matter of minutes he and his horse were floundering desperately in the quicksand. The Negro servant tried to throw his bridle to his master but the reins were too short. He searched for a pole or a long branch but could find nothing. In an agony of helplessness he watched his young master and his horse sink beneath the sand.

The young girl was inconsolable. In her grief she walked endlessly along the strand. One afternoon when a Northeast wind blew a fine spray across the beach she saw the figure of a man standing looking out over the water. He was dressed in gray and as she approached him and he became more distinct, her heart began to pound violently. She was only a few feet from him and now she was certain it was her dead lover who stood before her. Then a mist seemed to swirl up from the sea and wrap itself about him. He was gone.

When she told her family of the occurrence, they looked at each other sadly. They could only believe that the shock of her loss was beginning to affect her mind.

That night she had a dream so frighteningly vivid that she ran to her father's room for comfort. She had dreamed she was in a tiny boat tossed to and fro by heavy seas. All about her floated pieces of wreckage. And on a high sand dune, which she was helpless to reach, stood her lover beckoning her toward him.

The next day the girl's father decided to carry his daughter to a renowned Charleston physician. The entire family accompanied them. Within hours after they had left the Inlet tragedy struck. A savage hurricane swooped down upon the coast. For two days the storm raged like a monster run amuck.

When it was finally over news came that almost the entire population of North Inlet had perished. Homes were swept out to sea before the inhabitants were able to escape. The savage storm of 1822 had come and gone and the disaster would be remembered for many a year.

By now the fortunate young lady realized that the appearance of her lover and the dream had saved her life as well as the lives of the members of her family. Resigned at last to the loss of her fiancé, she became her normal self again. Although this took place over a century ago many of the natives of the island are convinced the Gray Man still returns.

If you should happen to be walking along the strand and encounter a misty figure dressed in gray—remember, he brings a warning.

Tsali, the Cherokee Brave

HE GAVE HIS LIFE FOR HIS PEOPLE, AND HIS GHOST STILL WALKS THE MOUNTAIN PEAKS WHICH WERE ONCE HIS HOME

When the harvest moon pours its rays over the mist shrouded peaks of the Great Smoky Mountains, men swear they see the ghostly figure of an Indian striding the leafy trails or silhouetted for an instant against the sky as though gazing across the deep shadowed valleys.

Thus read a dispatch of the Associated Press on August 3, 1940. The story appeared in the *Charlotte*

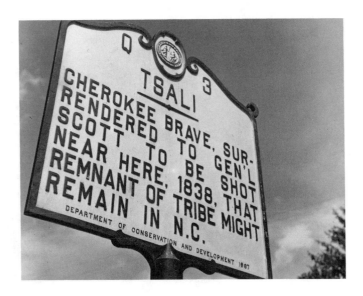

Observer and other North Carolina newspapers on the wire service.

Few people knew the Indian's name. It was Tsali. He had been a brave in the powerful Cherokee nation a century before. His home was on the Little Tennessee River not far from the village of Echota, a Cherokee capital near the North Carolina-Tennessee border where the mountains thrust themselves 6,000 feet up into the sky. It is here that the spirit of Tsali roams. And those of his people who dwell there today do so only because of him.

The ghost of Tsali has been seen now for more than a hundred years. No one can say when it first appeared or how often it has been seen. But his story is part of a sad and ugly chapter in our history.

In Tsali's time the Cherokee nation extended across and beyond the great mountains. The boundaries had been set in war with the Powhatan, Monacan, Tuscarora, Catawba, Creek, Chickasaw, and Shawano. After the defeat of the Creek and Shawano, the Cherokee lands extended from upper Georgia to the Ohio River and included hunting grounds in Kentucky.

But from the East came white settlers pushing steadily farther into the Cherokee territory. In 1777, just a year after the Declaration of Independence was signed, the North Carolina legislature offered a bounty of land to able bodied men who would fight the Cherokee. Of course, this land was to come from the Indians.

At that time Tennessee was still part of North Carolina. Among the men who came forward to fight the Indians was Colonel John Sevier. (Later he led his men in a vital victory over the British at King's Mountain.) Another young man named Andrew Jackson also joined the campaign. When peace finally came again and treaties were signed, The Cherokee saw much of their land taken away.

But it wasn't the desire for farm land or the settlers moving West that finally sounded the death knell of the Cherokee nation. Its fate was sealed the day an Indian boy found a yellow stone in a creek near the present site of Dahlonega, Georgia. His mother polished it and showed it to a white trader. The "stone" was gold.

Like a pestilence the cry spread: "There's gold on the Cherokee land!"

Old treaties were forgotten and a new treaty was signed in 1817 and approved by President James Monroe. It provided for removing the Cherokee from the Great Smoky Mountains to the Territory of Oklahoma. After all, the Cherokee didn't "need" gold and there was other land out beyond the Mississippi where they could hunt.

Rage swept the Cherokee nation. War drums echoed across haze filled valleys. Then the white men, faced by certain conflict, backed down and years of bickering followed. At last they agreed to pay the Cherokees five million dollars for their land—the land of the sky.

It was a warm spring day in May of 1838 when General Winfield Scott marched into Cherokee country at the head of seven thousand troops. He delivered an ultimatum to the Cherokee chiefs. They and their people must "move West before the new moon."

The soldiers set about building stockades and rounding up Indians. Cattle were shot. Families were seized, many while they were eating. Some were not even given time to gather up their possessions. What was to be an orderly move turned into a debacle. Perhaps it was a miscarriage of orders, or maybe lower ranking officers who hated the Indians abused their authority—who can say? But the effect was disastrous.

By the time the first group of Indians reached the banks of the Mississippi there was ice in the river. There were no shelters, no blankets. The soldiers

didn't provide them. Before the Indians reached Oklahoma four thousand of them were dead. It was one of the most shameful episodes in American history.

When the move westward started, Tsali was living in the Ocono Luftee Valley with his wife, three children, and a brother. Three soldiers seized Tsali as he worked in a field near his home. He and his family were led down the mountain to a stockade. The soldiers planned to keep them there until they had rounded up all the Indians. Then they would herd them toward Oklahoma.

As the group made their way along the trail one of the soldiers prodded Tsali's wife to walk faster. Tsali called out something in the Cherokee tongue to his sons and they attacked the guards . In the scuffle a rifle went off and one of the soldiers fell dead. The others ran.

Tsali and his family fled back into the high mountains. The mountains were their home and they would not leave them. Other Cherokee families were doing the same. But the guards reported that Tsali had killed a soldier and General Scott was determined not to let any Indian who killed a white man go free.

The General knew it would cost him many men to capture Tsali among the mountains and that the remaining Cherokees would fight to the death before allowing themselves to be taken.

So Scott called on a white trader named William Thomas to find Tsali. The General must have felt that Tsali had a sense of honor for he made him an offer:

"Tell Tsali that if he will come down and give himself up the rest of his people can stay in the great mountains."

Thomas was a trusted trader and friend of the Indians. They took him to Tsali.

It was one life for a thousand. If Tsali gave himself up the General would leave the mountains in peace. The Indians who had escaped the troops would be free to live in the Smokies forever. The chief of the white man's army would pledge this.

Tsali accepted the offer and came down from the mountains. The Indians were left in peace as Scott had promised, but the price was Tsali's life. He was shot by a firing squad.

It was a score of years before troops again forced their way into the North Carolina mountains. These were blue clad men under Stoneman and they were cutting east through the mountains in an effort to free Union prisoners at Salisbury. The cavalry pickets may have been nervous, for several reported seeing the silhouette of an Indian brave walking along the ridge in the moonlight. They fired but their echoing shots struck nothing.

For a hundred years now there has been peace in the valleys of the Smokies. But if you don't believe that Tsali still strides proudly along the trails, go there when the harvest moon pours its rays on the mist of an autumn night.

Go where there is no highway, where the mountains are high. Watch there for the figure of an Indian silhouetted tall against the sky.

Litchfield Plantation near All Saints Church near Georgetown, South Carolina, is one of the oldest plantations in the area. It is still beautifully preserved. The ghost of Litchfield who returns to haunt it is one of its former owners. He was a doctor who lived and died here before the Civil War. Later owners of the plantation and the Negroes who lived on it have seen him many times.

The Ghost of Litchfield

Occupants of Litchfield Plantation have been awakened many a night by the noisy shade of a former owner

The wooden gates and the bell post are gone now, replaced by more durable iron. But still told are stories of the kindly doctor who returns to his beloved Litchfield. His visits are made at night, or very occasionally on a dreary, gray day.

When the doctor was alive he would ride up to the plantation gate on a handsome bay and strike the bell, which had no clapper, with the handle of his riding crop. The doctor kept the gates of his plantation locked. But nearby lived a gatekeeper whose responsibility it was to hear the bell and let him in. Sometimes the gatekeeper would slip away on a visit to a neighboring plantation. When this happened the tired doctor would beat the bell furiously and no one would answer.

He would finally tie his horse to the bell post, climb over a split log fence, and walk down the long avenue of oaks to the house. After late calls he would use the small, pri-

vate stairway to his room to avoid disturbing the family.

Long after the doctor's death owners of Litchfield would hear the clanging of the bell at all hours of the night as it did when the doctor returned from his calls. Sometimes he would suddenly appear in the house or on the dark little back stairs. But most often he would make his presence known by the clamorous ringing of the bell. Finally, one owner decided he would have his slumbers disturbed no longer. He ordered the bell removed.

He made no secret of the fact that he didn't care how often the good doctor returned but he was tired of being waked up in the dead of night by the bell at the gate.

If you should pass Litchfield late at night and see a bay tethered there in the shadows—you may be sure the doctor has come home again.

City of Death

A COURAGEOUS DOCTOR FINALLY MET THE SHAPELESS EVIL THAT PROWLED THE STREETS OF THE STRICKEN CITY

The port town of Nassau was an exciting, polyglot place in the summer of 1862. There were swaggering blockade runner captains with more money in their pockets than a governor could earn in a year. There were boisterous free Negroes, and there were the islanders themselves who as far back as anyone could remember had earned an unsavory livelihood from pillaging the wrecks washed up on their shores.

It was the last of August when something unseen and full of horror left the island with the crew of the steamer *Kate*, bound for the port of Wilmington, North Carolina. Even if the sailors had been celebrating less heavily before their departure they could hardly have been aware of their fearsome stowaway that was soon to bring tragedy to the people of Wilmington.

The dead might have described it better for us than those fortunate enough to escape. But perhaps we may come to know its gruesome presence through the eyes of a man who during that ill-fated month of September was still alive.

Dr. James H. Dickson, shoulders bent from exhaustion, closed the door of the small house which

looked out over the waterfront of the Wilmington harbor. The child he had been treating for several days lay dead in the tiny room he had just left. And as in so many other cases he had visited during the past week, he had been helpless to combat the relentless torment of the yellow fever that had killed his patient.

The disease was a new one to all Wilmington physicians. Municipal authorities were helpless and the country people, fearful of the dread fever, no longer sent in supplies.

Skilled physician that he was, Dickson went end-lessly on his rounds, often to the bedside of close friends, only to watch them die. The socially promi-nent and the humble poor alike tossed, suffered, and went out by the same door, while rude funeral carts rumbled in the streets and carried them all to the same destination.

Although heavy hearted over the ravages of the fever, James Dickson was almost equally disturbed over *the rumor*. As the number of deaths mounted the frightened slaves had started whispers of an accom-panying horror, a nameless, faceless thing, an em-bodiment of evil which roamed the deserted streets and carried with it the touch of death.

A pall of black smoke from the burning barrels of tar designed to purify the air hung over the city and obscured the early morning light.

"Truly an infernal setting for an evil spirit, if such existed, at large in this panic stricken city," thought James Dickson. A man of calmness and logic, it was with determination that he shook off his sombre mood. Such superstitious imaginings could only stem from the fears of the illiterate.

At that moment a gust of wind rustled through the bushes at the edge of the street along which he walked and blew choking black billows toward him from one of the tar barrels. He felt something soft like a cloak brush his face. But as he reached out involun-tarily to ward it off his hand met empty air. For a moment his throat almost closed with an unaccustomed emotion—fear.

When he recovered himself he searched the bushes but found nothing. He noted only the now still leaves of the trees as his eyes searched for some other living thing.

As he neared the large magnolia tree in his own yard he saw shadows moving by the steps of his house. Nerving himself to walk toward them he recognized a human figure. It was an old man whose whole body was racked by barely suppressed sobs.

Deeply moved, Dickson asked if he could help him.

"Doctor, it's not me. It's my daughter. In God's name, you've got to help her—she has the fever." And so incoherent did he become that Dickson could hardly understand where the old fellow lived.

On the way he gathered that the family's name was Fairly. The girl was their only daughter. Her husband had died a week ago at Sharpsburg. They entered a modest frame house. The mother's face was drawn but controlled as she led them to her daughter's room.

Dickson looked in the slight form of the girl lying beneath the sheet. She had been hemorrhaging badly and he knew it was already too late. He administered what little comfort he could, proscribed fruit juices although tortured by the knowledge that the family probably couldn't obtain them due to the blockade, and left. By now almost totally exhausted, he went home and threw himself across his bed.

Another day dawned and the doctor's rounds began anew. Here and there as he left a home a member of the family would accompany him to the door and with an air of embarrassment whisper, "Doctor, they say there is something roaming the streets at night. Tell me, have you seen anything?" And the slaves would listen fearfully, the whites of their eyes shining from the darkness along the edges of the hall.

If Dickson had not been so busy his own imagination, spurred on by fatigue, might have run more

rampant. But he would not, could not stop although his own frustration and helplessness lashed him at every bedside. At the home of the Lassiters young James followed him to the door and asked, "Is it true that 'The Thing' got Ben Trumbell last night and left him dead in the street without a mark on his body?"

Dickson merely shook his head tiredly without further reply. When he got home that night his head ached miserably but he decided an account must be written of the cases for future record.

He sat alone in his little office at the back of the house slumped over his roll top desk, the window open at his side. He wrote on and on until his fingers felt cramped. By now his entire body ached and he realized that these were the first symptoms of the pestilence. The curtain stirred softly at the window.

By Friday he was unable to make his calls. But again that night, despite his increasing weakness, he wrote one page after another. The hand writing was somewhat less legible but still bold and unflinching. An unusual chill was in the wind for September and it ruffled his papers.

On Saturday night as he sat at his desk it seemed to him the odor of the tar barrels was more pungent than ever. The wind which now began to blow the curtain aside was almost icy. But his face burned so with the fever that he welcomed it—nay, if there was some presence beyond the blackness of the window which could end all this, he sought it.

With all his remaining strength he turned and stared through the now parted curtains. Strangely enough he recognized what he saw there. It was what he had brushed past that night early in the epidemic, The Thing that every man wonders how he will meet.

Now it was to be his companion beneath the black

pall of smoke, his dark escort past the blazing barrels of pitch through the silent streets.

In the *Wilmington Journal* of September 29, 1862, an inconspicuous notice appeared, "Dr. James H. Dickson, a physician of the highest character and standing, died here early Sunday morning of yellow fever. Dr. Dickson's death is a great loss to the profession and to the community."

Treasure Hunt

THE FURY OF BATTLE SEEMED ALMOST TAME TO TWO YOUNG OFFICERS AFTER THEIR GHOSTLY ENCOUNTER ON FOLLY ISLAND

In 1908 in Deadwood, South Dakota, a little book was published by a former Union Army officer. Francis M. Moore had served with distinction during the war between the states but the subject of his book was not a narrative of battles. It was an eerie tale of a search for buried treasure on Folly Island near Charleston harbor.

For half a century those who knew the story were sworn to secrecy. In July of 1863 the 62nd Ohio Regiment was part of a Union force under General Gilmore. The men landed on Folly Island in preparation for an attack on the defenses of Charleston harbor. Before the fighting was to start Gilmore ordered the Negroes living on the island removed and provided a steamer to take them to Port Royal.

A young lieutenant named Yokum, who was supervising one of the details, walked up to a ramshackle cabin occupied by an old Negro woman and a child. When he informed her she would have to leave the island she protested vehemently. The lieutenant, trying to be as kind as possible, sat on the porch and listened to her talk while the child brought him a drink of spring water in a gourd.

The Negress told Yokum how her family had lived

in the cabin while pirates still roamed the Carolina coast. Judging that her age must be close to a hundred, he became convinced she was telling the truth as her story appeared to be from first hand experience.

When she mentioned buried treasure the words cut through the oppressive July heat and aroused a spark of interest in the young officer.

"Six chests of gold, silver and jewels were carried ashore by the pirates. They dug a hole for it between dem two big oaks." And she pointed a figure as gnarled as the trees themselves. Her voice dropped almost to a whisper as she told how the frightened Negroes had watched.

As the last chest was lowered into the hole the leader of the buccaneers suddenly stabbed one of his men in the back and tumbled him into the opening. Quickly the other pirates shoveled sand over the body and soon they had vanished back to the sea from whence they had come.

It was not long before a large ship appeared on the horizon, apparently in search of the pirates. From her description Lieutenant Yokum guessed that it might have been a British man of war.

He was now intensely interested.

"I suppose the treasure has been dug up long since?" he asked with only a trace of hope in his voice.

"No suh, no suh. Who gonna go near dat place? Dat pirate he watch over dem chests even do' he dead." And the old woman fell silent, looking out toward the sea. Yokum helped her carry her few belongings down to the boat and she and the child boarded it along with the other Negroes.

That night shortly before twelve o'clock two officers of the 62nd Ohio, each equipped with a shovel, disappeared over the sand dunes. Yokum and his friend, Lieutenant Hatcher, had no trouble finding the giant live oaks which grew a short distance from the Negro cabin. They were shrouded with Spanish moss and so much taller than the other trees on the narrow strip of land that they stood out conspicuously.

As they neared their goal the tops of the trees began to rustle and stir although there was no breeze and the air hung still and heavy with heat.

Taking their bearings and choosing a site directly between the two oaks, which were about twenty feet apart, the men began to dig. There was a flash of lightning and Yokum looked up at the sky for signs of a summer thunderstorm. To his surprise no distant roll of thunder followed. Hatcher pointed to the tops of the trees now swaying and writhing as if buffeted by a strong wind.

They raised their shovels and resumed digging. The sand which the wind swept against their faces and bare torsos stung like thousands of tiny needles. But they continued to dig. By now the darkness was illuminated by numerous flashes of lightning and at times they could see each other as plainly as if it were day.

Then a flash came which seemed to last for several seconds. The area where they dug became bright as noonday. At that moment a shattering realization came to both men.

They were not alone.

There was someone or something standing there beside them. Was it human? The figure was one that neither of them would ever be able to forget. It was clearly that of a pirate.

Yokum and Hatcher waited for no introduction. They fled in panic over the dunes and back toward their camp. When they reached its safety the two men swore to each other that they would not tell of their experience.

The following day the 62nd attacked Morris Island. Hatcher and Yokum fought with a calmness and valor that astonished their comrades. Perhaps they did so with a sense of relief that their enemies were mere mortals. Then came the assault on Fort Wagner and Fort Fisher. Both men were decorated for bravery.

Even at the end of the war the story of that night on the beach remained untold. A few years later Hatcher had died and Yokum had gone out West to make his home.

It was not until fifty years after the war that Yokum related their experience at a veterans' reunion. It was recorded by his friend, Francis M. Moore, and should make interesting reading for all who are tempted to wrest buried treasure from its owners!

House of the Opening Door

WHY DID THE DOOR OPEN EACH NIGHT WITHOUT BENEFIT OF HUMAN HAND? FEW CARED TO STAY LONG ENOUGH TO FIND OUT

A house is more than just its timbers. It is the lives which have been lived there, the deeds which have been done within its walls. There are houses which finally can only be at home in hell itself. If you glimpse one on your travels do not tarry. It may prove a trap of terror, a passport to the damned.

But the couple who sat in their ancient auto looking hopefully at the gaunt structure rising before them did not think of these things. If they had been told they might not have cared. For they were desperate. All John and Harriet West could think of was that they had at last found shelter for themselves and their four children.

Harriet gazed at the tangle of dead vines hanging over the porch, writhing at the touch of the wind. And she was foolish enough to picture clematis growing in their place. Devil's Walking Stick might have thrived on this God-forsaken spot—but flowers . . . never.

John's eyes looked beyond the grotesque, broken trees which must once have been giants and day-dreamed of an apple orchard. What did these two outsiders care for the strange expressions on the faces of the North Carolina mountain people whom they

had stopped to ask the way to the house? It was enough for them that it had four walls and a roof.

Harriet and John West stood in the front yard of the place they expected to call home, their coats whipped around them by the wind, two silhouettes in the falling dusk. Behind them their children peered curiously from the car windows, quiet now that the journey was over. Then the entire family began the work of unloading the small canvas covered trailer which held their meager household goods.

That night the children were exhausted and needed no urging to go to their floor pallets. Soon they were slumbering soundly.

John and his wife worked on. He had discovered a few boards at the back of the house, the last of a tumbled down shed, and chopped some wood which hissed and crackled in the big stone fireplace. Shortly before midnight they pulled their chairs close to the hearth and began to talk of their plans for fixing up their new home.

The fire cast strange shadows on the broken plaster of the walls. The vines scraped eerily as the wind blew them back and forth against the outside of the house. The Wests were too absorbed to notice either.

Then they both started. Above the steady wail of the wind came an earsplitting sound. It was the shriek of a train whistle echoing and re-echoing through the night. Hardly a mile from where the house stood, a stretch of railroad track ran through a narrow gap between two hills. Before the train entered the straightaway beyond the gap its engineer blew a long shrill blast of the whistle which was answered and echoed back and forth all down the corridor formed by the hills.

It was not a comforting thing to hear and the Wests looked at each other, wordlessly waiting for what might follow. When it came they were still unprepared. At the far end of the room was a door leading to the long ell which ran back of the two story part of the house. Back there had originally been a kitchen and small servant's room. The Wests had decided to close this room off, keeping it as a storage place for farm tools, and use only the front part of the house.

But someone or something had decided differently. Something that was not to be closed in or perhaps kept out. As the man and woman watched, frozen with apprehension, the knob on the door seemed to turn slowly. They heard the latch click and then a crack appeared between the door and the door jamb. So slight it was that one at first might only have imagined it to be there. But the streak of velvety blackness widened with horrifying deliberation until at last the entire black maw of the door gaped at the pair sitting before the fire.

For a long moment neither moved. Then came a sharp crash as if some large object had been hurled savagely through the air against the wall in the pitch black storage room.

John West jumped to his feet, grasped a candle and hesitating only for a moment at the door of the room disappeared inside it. Harriet watched as the flickering candle stretched faltering fingers of light over the walls and across the floor. There was no living thing to be seen. The room was empty and everything seemed undisturbed. Almost everything, that is. On the floor lay a large scythe—its sharp, wickedly curved blade shining in the semi-darkness.

John West picked it up quickly and hung it back on the wall, then turned to his wife: "Well, you can see for yourself it was nothing. Only the scythe falling from the wall. We're both tired and jumpy. Tomorrow you won't give an old door with a loose catch a thought."

Harriet West looked at her husband, her eyes still frightened. But she said nothing. It was now after midnight, and they went on to bed. Soon Harriet was asleep, but not her husband. He knew he had hung the scythe securely over hooks on the wall of the storage room and go over it as he would in his mind he knew of no way it could have fallen to the floor— particularly since it had come to rest fully ten feet from where he had hung it.

The next day the opening door and the chilling fear which had accompanied it seemed like only a bad dream to be dissipated by the sunlight. And only now and then did a nagging uneasiness about the scythe touch the mind of John West as he busied himself with minor repairs to the wretched, run-down old house. The latch of the door to the storage room appeared to be more than secure. In fact it was even a bit difficult to open, being rusty from years of disuse.

Shortly after supper the children went to bed exhausted from exploring every nook and cranny of the house and the land around it.

John and Harriet West were tired, too. But neither would admit to it, nor to the fact that they were both waiting. For a while they talked. Then they were too tired even for that. Finally Harriet's head came to rest on her husband's shoulder. By now it was almost midnight.

Then the sound they had been waiting for came. Louder, eerier than ever the scream of the train's whistle broke the stillness and behind it came the rumble, rumble, rumble of the freight cars rushing down the straightaway. Both stared tensely at the door and as they watched it began to open once again. Harriet gripped John's hand, her face white with fear. The door hung wide on its hinges. Now from somewhere in the blackness of the room beyond came a loud crash.

John West ran toward the door with Harriet close behind him. There in the light of the candle lay the scythe on the floor just as it had been the night before. This time when he picked it up he found to his horror that the blade bore a rusty—or was it reddish?—stain. It had struck the floor with such force that the board on which it rested was scarred.

As he passed his fingers over the mark the board moved and he saw that it was quite loose. So loose that he could easily lift it. Peering under it, John West saw to his surprise an old metal box. The box was wedged in so tightly that it was only with the help of his crowbar that West managed to pry it out. Taking the box into the other room in front of the fire, they both worked at the lock. Finally, John struck it with the crowbar and the lock sprang open.

What John and Harriet were to find inside that box was to change their whole lives. It was a turning point they would never be able to forget or explain.

The lid of the box still held fast to its secret John worked the crowbar around its edge impatiently until all at once it gave way, flying back with such suddenness that the contents of the box spilled over onto the floor. The pair gasped with amazement. For a moment both were speechless. Stacked inside the box and spilling over onto the floor around it was more money than they had ever seen in their lives.

This was no pirate's treasure of gold doubloons, but musty old bills—currency which must have been stacked away long years before. Sitting on the floor they counted the money a half dozen times, their hands shaking with excitement, before they realized that they had discovered well over ten thousand dollars.

They talked until the early hours of the dawn of how they would spend their find, before at last they fell asleep. They would buy a small farm, they would have a cow so the children could have all the milk they wanted. Harriet would be able to get some chickens and John could buy a horse with which to plow.

But however the Wests would eventually spend their treasure, one thing was certain. They would never spend another night listening for the shriek of the train and waiting in dread for the ell door to open. By early the next afternoon the house was again alone with its secrets. The Wests were gone.

As the years went by an occasional family would stay in the house on the hill for a few nights and leave. Even tramps were not brave enough to spend more than a night or two in the "house of the opening door."

The strange story of the house and its door spread until it reached the ears of a young engineer. He was able to interest a group in solving the mystery and they came with their tape measures and their instruments to examine the house and surrounding area with scientific thoroughness. For two weeks they stayed, watching as the door opened. They were convinced that there is nothing in the world that will not allow itself to be measured and categorized.

Despite their air of skepticism more than one felt a strange sense of foreboding when midnight approached. One slipped a loaded pistol into his pocket while his friends laughed at his precaution.

As each midnight drew near the blasts of the train whistle pierced the air and rebounded between the hills. Then the door would swing open slowly, finally to rest against the wall. There was certainly a scientific explanation, the men believed, and so they studied and argued over the problem, taking voluminous notes and sitting before the fire night after night. Finally they decided they had solved the mystery. This is what they wrote in their report:

"The mountains of Western North Carolina are the oldest in the world. At one time they stretched across what is now the Pacific Ocean, to join this country with Japan. In these old, old mountains are many peculiar geologic formations—strange strata of rock which are found in few other mountain ranges. We would call attention to the fact that on many of the mountain tops there are found bold flowing springs.

"The structure locally known as the House of the Opening Door rests on a hill of almost solid rock, the soil in some places a few feet thick, and in others only scant inches. The midnight train which passes through every night at almost the same time is the heaviest freight going over this route. It has a clear track, for there are no other trains passing near this time, and its rate of speed is unchecked. The terrific weight and velocity of this train jars a certain stratum of rock as it makes the curve just before reaching the straight sweep in to the water tank at the station. By an unusual, perhaps remarkable coincidence, the House of the Opening Door rests on the same vein and stratum of rock and the vibrations are carried from one point to the other.

"The opening door has been measured very carefully and we find that it does not hang exactly true, so the trembling shock imparted to the layer of rock by the heavy train is carried in successive waves to the stout foundation under that part of the house. The trembling is sufficient to swing the door."

Thus was the mystery of the opening door disposed of scientifically.

When the natives heard the results of the report they merely shook their heads. It might be that the men with the "book larnin" had discovered the door's secret, but no one cared to stay in the house overnight to find out.

Then an old man and his son who had been burned out of their own home decided they would spend a night in the house to find out whether they wanted to move in.

They awoke just in time to see the door swing open and hear a noise like the shuffling of feet in the other room. Then from the blackness of the open doorway something shiny came hurtling through the air and landed perilously close to the younger man's head. Both father and son jumped up and fled out into the night.

A year later a group of children wandered near the house in play. One of the girls peeked through a window heavy with cobwebs and there in the middle of the room in a streak of sunlight stood a ragged old man. Under one arm he cradled something which might have been a box and in his other hand he held a knife which he plunged fiercely into the air. The child screamed and the old man vanished.

For a long time now the house has stood empty. Its appearance grows more grim year by year. But still it waits on its lonely hill in western North Carolina with the broken off trees looming like lost souls around it. If you care to spend the night there you have the reassuring report of the engineers.

But local people say it would do no good to nail the door shut or plaster over it for "what comes through that door will not be shut out or closed in. When the time comes it will be there—door or no door".

Some years back Eugene F. LaBruce, member of a prominent Georgetown, South Carolina family, gave the following account of his experience with the "Ghosts of Hagley."

The Ghosts of Hagley

On a moonlit night in 1918 a Georgetown man learned that phantoms still walk the earth

It was in the summer of 1918 that I under went an experience destined to change all of my preconceived ideas about the spirit world . . . An experience which convinced me beyond the shadow of a doubt that ghosts do walk the earth.

I never recall having any fear of ghosts and like most people thought they were merely products of an overwrought imagination. But the peculiar events of that summer demonstrated very plainly that I was wrong.

At the time, I was engaged in carrying passengers between Pawley's Island and the ferry landing of Hagley. Between the Island and the landing was a sandy road several miles long. Using a large automobile, I would make the trip a number of times during the day. Often a party of young people who worked in Georgetown would hire a gasoline launch after the ferry had made its last trip and I would meet them at Hagley about a quarter of eleven.

One night when I reached the ferry landing early I decided to stretch out on a piece of canvas on the wharf and get a little rest before the boat from Georgetown arrived. The moon shone brightly, flooding the landscape with its soft light, and every object was plainly visible. It was a peaceful scene and a few minutes later I had drifted off to sleep.

The dream that came to me that night was so vivid that I can remember every detail to this day.

I was standing with a crowd of people in front of a little church near the wharf. A wedding was in progress and it seemed that we were waiting for the bride and groom to emerge from the front door. Everyone wore clothing typical of the Civil War period, and I gathered that peace had just been declared. After a short while the bridal party appeared on the church porch. I stared at the newly married couple standing there in the moonlight and noticed that the bride was a striking brunette, and the groom a handsome, finely proportioned blond. Both were of the landed gentry class, I imagined.

As the crowd surged toward the porch a man dressed in Confederate uniform dashed up to the clearing astride a horse that had evidently been running at top speed for hours. The figure dismounted and ran toward the place where the bride and groom stood. When he reached the couple the bride uttered a little cry and said, "It is too late, I have just been married!"

The soldier stood frozen and listened like a man in a trance while the woman explained that she had waited three years, and believing that he had been killed in battle had finally consented to marry one of her former beaus.

The soldier then turned to the groom and said, without show of emotion, "Then I will fade out of the picture—it is the only solution." And he turned to leave. But the groom started after him. "No! If it must be one of us, I will be the one." Followed by the bride and groom the soldier made for the wharf. When he reached the end of the pier he jumped off and disappeared. Without a second's hesitation, the woman in white followed him and then the groom.

Everyone was in a turmoil. Boats were launched, the stronger swimmers among the men jumped into the water and a score of men were calling orders in rapid succession. A severe gale had begun blowing from the west lashing the waves against the bank. The search for the bodies was still under way when I awoke, shivering with excitement.

I rubbed my eyes and looked about me. The church had disappeared and the crowd of men and women had vanished. It scarcely seemed like a dream, I had witnessed the entire train of events so clearly and with such detail. But it must have been for I was back on the wharf. Only one thing had changed. I was no longer alone.

For as I turned my head I saw two figures standing only a few feet away. And to my amazement they were dressed like the people in my dream, the woman resembling the bride and the man, the groom!

"This is nonsense," I assured myself. "The boat has come and gone and the passengers are somewhere nearby. These two are trying to play a trick on me." So I said, most politely, "Will you tell me who you are? If you are waiting to go to Pawley's I have the automobile ready."

They did not answer so I tried again. Neither deigned to reply, but turned around and strolled off the dock. This made me angry and I called out, "You better stop this foolishness and tell me who you are, for I will find out soon enough."

But the couple kept walking slowly away from me

seemed to be whispering to each other. Then I came really frightened and started to imagine all sorts of weird things. Could some mysterious force have carried me back through the years to the time of the Civil War? I tried to recall the history of this area but couldn't remember ever hearing of a church at Hagley, reading of such an incident or hearing a similar story told. Why, then, should I have this dream?

I was still trying to answer these questions when the couple disappeared. I had been watching them intently and was sure they had no opportunity to slip into the woods. They had simply melted away without a trace.

Scarcely had I collected my wits when the motor boat arrived with its passengers. I tried my best to conceal my agitation as they followed me to the automobile and we were soon ploughing along the sandy roadbed headed for the beach. The car was in second gear traveling at about twenty miles an hour when I saw two figures step out into the road directly in front of the machine. With no clearance on either side of the car there was nothing to do but slam on the brakes.

So sudden was the stop that my passengers were thrown violently against each other and started calling, "What are you trying to do, throw us out of the car?"

Cold perspiration broke out on my face. The figures were still in the road walking arm in arm and there was the brunette bride of my dream and the handsome groom. There was no mistaking their features or the costumes. They did not even throw a glance in the direction of the car and I was sure no living beings could have failed to notice the automobile bearing down upon them.

Here are my ghosts again, " I said to myself. "Perhaps I am going mad."

"What's the matter?" yelled a young man in a sporty blue coat "Have you lost your voice? That was a fine trick."

"Oh, I just thought I would throw you and your girl friend together," I replied. When I looked back at the road the figures were gone. I was afraid the girl at my side would notice my agitation but she seemed absorbed in her own thoughts.

When we reached the beach my passengers alighted—all except the girl who was seated next to me. She seemed reluctant to leave and when her companions called to her she said, "All of you run

along, I want to talk to Eugene a while." So they laughed but moved on down the beach.

The girl turned to me. "Eugene, I want you to tell me why you stopped the car so suddenly by the ferry landing."

"Oh, I just wanted to have a little fun," I replied trying to stick to my original story.

"You needn't tell me that. I know why you stopped."

My heart was beating faster and faster. Perhaps this young woman had seen the same figures. In this case nothing was the matter with my mind and probably two real ghosts had appeared.

"Why don't you believe me?" I countered.

"Because," and she averted her eyes, "you know you saw a man and a woman in the road."

"If we did, no one else in the car saw them," I asserted.

"That makes no difference. I saw them and you did, too, or you would never have slammed on the brakes as you did."

There was no use pretending any longer. "Yes, I saw them," I said evenly, "and I barely missed killing them at that." I knew that was not an accurate statement for the car would probably not have injured the couple a bit. They would have dissolved in front of my eyes. But I was determined not to frighten the girl.

But who were they, Eugene?" she persisted. "I never remember seeing them around here before, and did you notice those odd old fashioned clothes they wore?"

"Perhaps strangers out for a stroll, waiting to meet another car," I told the eager questioner.

But I knew better. I had seen two ghosts—the real thing. The fact that this girl and I had both seen the same apparitions left no doubt in my mind that spirits do exist and that we had been granted a rare privilege.

For all I know the beautiful bride and her groom may still stroll the wooded paths around the ferry landing at Hagley on bright moonlight nights.

Many stories have been written about old graveyards and countless legends have sprung up around them. One of these stories is still told in connection with the graveyard which lies south of historic St. James Episcopal Church in Wilmington, North Carolina, and the testimony put in writing is worth retelling. The facts were given by the late Colonel James G. Burr in a lecture which he delivered in the Wilmington Opera House on February 3, 1890.

Return from the Dead

A GOOD FRIEND IN LIFE CAME BACK FROM THE GRAVE TO REPROACH ALEXANDER HOSTLER FOR A HORRIBLE MISTAKE

Spring came very early that March of 1810 in Wilmington, North Carolina, but its loveliness passed unnoticed by Alexander Hostler. So grieved was Hostler by the death of his intimate friend, Samuel Jocelyn, that he shut himself up in his library wishing only to be alone.

To walk the streets and greet mutual friends or frequent the places which he and Samuel had enjoyed together was an almost unbearable experience. Son of a distinguished Wilmington lawyer, Jocelyn had been a most promising and charming young man. His death in an accident a few days before had greatly affected Hostler.

As Hostler sat alone in his library two days after the funeral he was startled from his brooding by the sudden appearance of a figure before him. To his astonishment he recognized his friend Jocelyn, who said to him, "How could you let me be buried when I was not yet dead?"

"Not dead?" exclaimed the horror stricken Alexander.

"No, I was not," replied Samuel. "Open my coffin and you will see that I am not lying on my back in the position in which you placed me." And the figure vanished.

Hostler, though greatly disturbed, believed that he must be the victim of a delusion brought on by the extreme shock and grief which he had suffered. He made every effort to rationalize his experience.

The next evening he sat again in his study. Scribbling away with a quill pen at his desk, he forced himself to perform the painful task of writing an account of Samuel's death to friends living some distance away.

He had been writing not more than half an hour when he was seized by an overwhelming prescience that something inexplicable was about to occur. Glancing up from his desk he was aghast to find the apparition of Jocelyn standing only a few feet away as it had on the previous evening. Again the ghost entreated him to open the coffin and again it vanished.

Hostler was much upset and when he closeted himself alone in his room on the following evening, he sat at his desk with considerable apprehension. It was less than an hour before he realized that he was not alone. There at his elbow stood the apparition this time beseeching him even more pitifully.

He could stand it no longer. His rationalizations were of no use to him and his state of mind was such that he determined to seek out his friend Louis Toomer that very night and ask for his help.

The two men talked until nearly midnight. Greatly concerned over Hostler's condition, Toomer tried his utmost to reassure him but his efforts were of no avail. Hostler's distressed mien and haggard appearance finally convinced Toomer that nothing would satisfy him but the opening of Jocelyn's grave.

So he consented to assist in the grisly task and they began to lay their plans. The disinterment must be done at night in order that they might accomplish it in the strictest secrecy. Toomer was to bring the shovels and enter the cemetery from the rear while Hostler was to provide a lantern. They agreed to meet at Jocelyn's grave at 11:30 the following evening.

The appointed night was overcast and only occasionally did the waning moon show itself from behind the shifting clouds. The graveyard was pitch dark when the men, talking in low tones, began their undertaking. Before long the moon peered down upon the gravediggers and cast its eerie glow on the headstones around them.

They dug silently on until with a thud Hostler's shovel struck the top of the coffin. Carefully they uncovered it and raised the lid. Both men stooped over it, turning the light of the lantern full upon the contents of the coffin. With a strangled cry Hostler threw his arm across his face.

There lay the body—face downward! In truth, young Samuel Jocelyn had been buried alive.

In order that as little publicity as possible might be given the tragic error both Hostler and Toomer made no general mention of their discovery. But Hostler confided in Colonel Burr's mother who was his near relative and Toomer told the facts of the disinterment in the presence of another venerable lady, Mrs. C. G. Kennedy, who put his statement in writing for Colonel Burr.

There have been many theories as to how such a thing could have happened. Jocelyn had been thrown from his horse while riding and was picked up and carried to his home in a comatose condition.

Then presumably dead, the body remained in the home for two days before it was interred in St. James churchyard. A newspaper writer in 1926 wrote:

"The assumption is that the fall from the horse brought on a state of catalepsy with accompanying muscular rigidity convincing everyone that the youth was dead."

Whatever the medical explanation for this appearance of death which resulted in the burial of a living man, the apparition itself is even more beyond our real of understanding.

Whistle While You Haunt

THE YOUNG MAN DIED A PAINFUL, LINGERING DEATH, BUT HE OFTEN RETURNS TO WHISTLE HIS FAVORITE MELODY

A cold, steady downpour of rain beat upon the stagecoach as it bumped and jerked along the cobblestone streets of Charleston. It was the year 1786 and for homesick Joseph Ladd Brown of Rhode Island, the first view of the city in which he was to spend the balance of his life was a dismal one.

He had chosen to settle in Charleston for reasons of health. But the night he had selected for his arrival was far from an auspicious omen.

The door to the coach opened and Joseph found the face of the driver thrust close to his own. The man was trying to tell him something above the sound of the storm. They had pulled up before a small tavern and the driver recommended that Joseph find lodging there for the night.

His relief that the trip was over soon fled, for the crowd within was a rowdy one. While the young doctor watched with growing distaste a well dressed man, clearly above the revelers about him, entered the tavern. He made his way to Joseph and introduced himself.

"I am Ralph Isaacs. You appear to be a stranger here and if you will forgive me for saying so, this is not a suitable lodging for a gentleman. Allow me to

guide you elsewhere."

Joseph thanked him gratefully and soon the two were on their way in Isaac's own carriage to a quiet, comfortable inn. As they drove along together they found much in common and the young doctor was impressed with Isaac's *savoir faire* and knowledge of the city.

Within a few days Joseph found permanent lodgings in the home of two sisters who were friends of General Nathanael Greene, a business associate of his father.

Gradually he began to build up a good medical practice in the city and his ability as a poet, together with his personal charm, combined to make him much sought after. The two elderly ladies became increasingly fond of their young boarder. And each afternoon they found themselves listening for his cheerful whistling as he bounded up the stairs. It was always the same tune—a quaint old English ballad—and when they heard it they knew he was in high good humor.

Joseph continued to see much of his friend Ralph Isaacs, but more and more Isaac's jealousy over the young doctor's popularity began to cloud their friendship. Ralph Isaacs had never attained the social prominence which was coming to Joseph so readily and his resentment grew.

One evening they attended the Shakespearean drama *Richard III* but they were not seated together since seating in theaters at that time was arranged in accordance with one's social standing. The actress, a Miss Barrett, was hopelessly inadequate and spoke her lines so softly that she could scarcely be heard.

On the way home the two men argued over the quality of the performance. And what had begun as a difference of opinion soon ended in a serious quarrel.

Dr. Brown took it upon himself to organize a protest of Isaac's conduct which was printed in the Charleston *Gazette*. In the letter to the newspaper Brown said, "I account it one of the misfortunes of my life that I became intimate with that man."

Isaacs fired back a bitter reply calling Brown "a self-created doctor and as blasted a scoundrel as ever disgraced humanity."

Brown's friends advised him that it was now a matter of honor which could only be settled by a challenge to a duel. The challenge was readily accepted and the duel was set for the following morning. Actually, Dr. Brown was reluctant to settle the matter in such a manner and wanted to call off the duel, but it was now too late.

Early the next morning the two antagonists examined their guns, stood back to back, paced the agreed upon twenty steps and turned face to face. Brown raised his pistol high and fired straight into the air—then stood motionless and waited. Isaacs was not so merciful. He fired his pistol twice, each time hitting Brown in the legs below the knees. He was determined to cripple the doctor for life.

The wounded young man was carried back to the

home of the sisters and for three weeks he lingered between life and death. Physicians were able to do little to alleviate his suffering and finally he died.

But the cheerful balled which he loved to whistle did not die with him. For it is said that the merry English tune and his bounding footsteps have been heard many times on the stairs of the old home at 59 Church Street.

The Brown Mountain Lights

SEEN AND INVESTIGATED FOR MORE THAN A CENTURY, A TANTALIZING MYSTERY REMAINS UNSOLVED IN THE MOUNTAINS OF NORTH CAROLINA

The brown Mountain Lights are one of the most famous of North Carolina legends. They have been reported a dozen times in newspaper stories. They have been investigated at least twice by the U.S. Geological Survey. And they have attracted the attention of numerous scientists and historians since the German engineer, Gerard William de Brahm, recorded the mysterious lights in the North Carolina mountains in 1771.

"The mountains emit nitrous vapors which are borne by the wind and when laden winds meet each other the niter inflames, sulphurates and deteriorates," said de Brahm. De Brahm was a scientific man and, of course, had a scientific explanation. But the early frontiersman believed that the lights were the spirits of Cherokee and Catawba warriors slain in an ancient battle on the mountainside.

One thing is certain, the lights do exist. They have been seen from earliest times. They appear at irregular intervals over the top of Brown Mountain—a long, low mountain in the foothills of the Blue Ridge. They move erratically up and down, visible at a distance but vanishing as one climbs the mountain. From Wiseman's View on Linville Mountain the

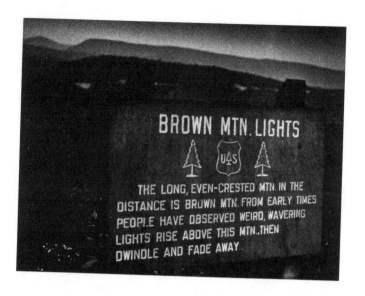

BROWN MTN. LIGHTS

THE LONG, EVEN-CRESTED MTN. IN THE
DISTANCE IS BROWN MTN. FROM EARLY TIMES
PEOPLE HAVE OBSERVED WEIRD, WAVERING
LIGHTS RISE ABOVE THIS MTN., THEN
DWINDLE AND FADE AWAY.

lights can be seen well. They at first appear to be about twice the size of a star as they come over Brown Mountain. Sometimes they have a reddish or blue cast. On dark nights they pop up so thick and fast it's impossible to count them.

Among the scientific investigations which have undertaken from time to time to explain the lights have been two conducted by the U.S. Geological Survey. The first was made in 1913 when the conclusion was reached that the lights were locomotive headlights from the Catawba Valley south of Brown Mountain. However, three years later in 1916 a great flood that swept through the Catawba Valley knocked out the railroad bridges. It was weeks before the right-of-way could be repaired and the locomotives could once again enter the valley. Roads were also washed out and power lines were down.

But the lights continued to appear as usual. It

became apparent that the lights could not be reflections from locomotive or automobile headlights.

The *Guide to the Old North State*, prepared by the W.P.A. in the 1930's, states that the Brown Mountain lights have puzzled scientists for fifty years." The same story reports sightings of the lights in the days before the Civil War.

Cherokee Indians were familiar with these lights as far back as the year 1200. According to Indian legend a great battle was fought that year between the Cherokee and Catawba Indians near Brown Mountain. The Cherokees believed that the lights were the spirits of Indian maidens who went on searching through the centuries for their husbands and sweethearts who had died in the battle.

There are innumerable stories of the lights. But perhaps the best description is that the lights are "a troop of candle-bearing ghosts who are destined to march forever back and forth across the mountain."

The lights can be seen from as far away as Blowing Rock or the Old Yonahlosse Trail over Grandfather Mountain some fifteen miles from Brown Mountain. At some points closer to Brown Mountain the lights seem large, resembling balls of fire from a Roman candle. Sometimes they may rise to various heights and fade slowly. Others expand as they rise, then burst high in the air like an explosion without sound.

Late in 1919 the question of the Brown Mountain lights was brought to the attention of th Smithsonian Institution and the United States Weather Bureau.

Dr. W. J. Humphries of the Weather Bureau investigated and reported that the Brown Mountain lights were similar to the Andes light of South America. The Andes light and its possible relation to the Brown Mountain lights became the subject of a paper read before the American Meteorological Society in April

1941. In this report Dr. Herbert Lyman represented the lights as a manifestation of the Andes light.

The second U.S. Geological Survey report disposes of the cause of the Brown Mountain lights by saying they are due to the spontaneous combustion of marsh gases. But there are no marshy places on or about Brown Mountain. The report also states that the lights from foxfire would be too feeble to be seen at a distance of several miles.

The report rules out the possibility that the lights are a reflection of mountain moonshine stills. "There are not enough such stills and they probably would not be in sufficiently continuous operation to produce lights in the number and regularity of those seen at Brown Mountain."

St. Elmo's Fire, that electrical phenomenon familiar to sea voyagers, was dismissed by a scientist from the Smithsonian Institution. He stated that St. Elmo's Fire and similar phenomena occurred at the extremity of some solid conductor and never in midair as in the case of the Brown Mountain lights.

Some scientists have advanced the theory that the lights are a mirage. Through some peculiar atmospheric condition they believe the glowing balls are reflections from Hickory, Lenoir and other towns in the area. The only drawback to this theory is that the lights were clearly seen before the War between the States, long before electricity was used to produce light.

In recent years scientists have been more concerned about exploring outer space. Perhaps they have forgotten that there are mysteries on our own planet still unsolved. The Brown Mountain lights are one of them.

The Hermitage, S. C.

Alice of the Hermitage

SHE DIED MORE THAN A HUNDRED YEARS AGO, BUT SHE STILL COMES BACK TO THE HOME SHE LOVED

It was one of the most elaborate balls of the Charleston season. A few short years before the coming of the War for Southern Independence, there was no hint of wartime austerity. Richly attired young men bowed before lavishly gowned girls in the sumptuous private ballroom. And soft music played on into the early morning hours.

One young girl stood our among the rest, lovely as a perfect camellia. Her flowing white gown, trimmed with lace and exquisitely embroidered, floated about her as she went through the figures of each dance with graceful perfection. No one could have guessed that when next the girl wore this dress she would be in her coffin.

Student at an exclusive young ladies' school in Charleston, Alice had been a reigning belle for two seasons. Shortly after the ball she was stricken with a fever thought to be malaria. Since it was near the end of the school term the head mistress decided to send her to her home at Murrell's Inlet north of Georgetown with a returning neighbor.

By the time Alice reached "The Hermitage," the family summer home built by her father in 1849, her condition was critical. Her malady was not malaria but the deadly typhoid. In spite of the loving care of her family she died within a few days.

The beautiful ball gown was unpacked and the wan but still lovely young girl was dressed in it for the last time. She had worn this same dress when a famous painter did her portrait, a portrait which could be seen in "The Hermitage" until recent years.

The body was placed in a glassed-in casket in Alice's own room and all who saw her exclaimed over her beauty even in death. At the time her mother was many miles away visiting relatives. No decision could be made as to a final resting place for the body so Alice was buried on the plantation. She was later removed to the churchyard and buried near relatives in the live-oak shaded cemetery.

It was not long after Alice's death that a Northern cousin arrived with her young son for a visit. The next morning at breakfast the boy asked who was the pretty lady in the white dress he had seen in his room. His mother told him that it had only been a dream. But the youngster steadfastly maintained that he had seen a girl who would not answer when he asked her name but only shook her head and smiled.

The hostess recognized his description as that of the girl who had died a few years before. A short time

Alice's bedroom at the Heritage

later Alice's apparition appeared in the garden to members of the family.

"The Hermitage" looks now much as it did at the time Alice lived there. For three generations she has continued to appear. Sometimes she walks through the garden in the moonlight. And on other occasions she may be seen sitting in the window of the room which was once her own. All who have seen her have been amazed at the beauty of this lovely young apparition who still returns to the home she loves so well.

The Night the Spirits Called

A GHOSTLY PLEA FOR HELP ADDED TO THE TERRORS OF THE STORMY NIGHT FOR THE CREW OF THE CAPE FEAR RIVER BOAT

Savage storms of sleet and snow are rare, indeed, in Wilmington, North Carolina. But not long after the Civil War a Christmas season came which was long remembered for its icy gales and inclement weather.

Broken branches and signs were strewn everywhere along the deserted streets. Many of the older buildings had been unroofed and torn by the fierce winds. Each day brought news of shipwrecks along the coast from Hatteras to Cape Fear. And every mail brought word of more lives lost at sea.

But the Southport mail boat *Wilmington* made her daily runs without a break, although there were times when the gale winds would toss her about until her upper rail was almost hidden by foam.

On December 24th there were indications that the weather would change. The *Wilmington* was due to sail at 5 o'clock and long before the warning whistle blew, a group of passengers bound for Southport boarded the boat with armloads of Christmas parcels. But before the steamer could leave the dock trouble had already begun. The voyage could not be made until a kettle in the engine room was mended. Captain Harper announced to his passengers that it would take at least six hours to repair the damage.

As darkness came the wind and snow increased. All the passengers but one decided to leave for more comfortable quarters on shore. Not averse to some sociability, the captain began to chat with his lone passenger. And soon the stranger began telling of colonial times.

"My great-grandfather was William McMillan of Edinburgh, who enlisted with the Camerons in the Rebellion of '45 and after the battle of Culloden was compelled to leave his country.

"He was a personal friend of Governor Gabriel Johnston of North Carolina. Johnston had invited him to come and make his home among the Cape Fear Scotsmen already settled in what is now Robeson county. On his way McMillan stopped at

Waddell's Ferry where he became an ardent Whig sympathizer. Many of his countrymen were here at the Ferry and they had never forgiven the British oppression.

"Unfortunately, McMillan and the two Highland Scots who had been marked as doomed men were captured by the cruel Tory Colonel, David Fanning. The Scots were to be put to death for their so-called treason in violating the oath of allegiance to the British crown—an oath reluctantly given which bound them to a hostile sovereign."

Fanning marched his prisoners to the town of Brunswick, now a ruin on Orton Plantation. Then he consigned the three men to the dank dungeons of an old prison ship which was anchored in the bay opposite Sugar Loaf Hill.

"After several agonizing and fruitless efforts to escape its gloomy hold they were brought to shore, given a mock trial and sentenced by Fanning to immediate execution. The place of execution was near Brunswick. Here the two Highlanders were bound together to a large pine tree.

"A platoon of unwilling soldiers drew up before them and fired. Their quivering, bleeding bodies were then unbound from the tree which it is said still marks the spot where these martyrs to freedom died. Then McMillan was brought forward, held by guards, to meet the same fate. But, an exceptionally powerful man, he struck one of them senseless, broke away from the other and managed to escape into the woods. From there he made his way back to Robeson county.

"The Orton people hold an old tradition that on stormy nights ghosts of the two Scotsmen walk abroad. They have also been seen on their phantom boat in search of rescuers."

By now the moaning wind and crackling sleet conspired to chill the flow of conversation. Harper had begun to think of the dangerous run ahead of him through the storm. It was almost midnight. But repairs were completed and the boat pulled away from the dock. The night was so thick that even the river lights were obscured. At times the Captain slowly felt his way without a guiding mark while the mate, Peter Jorgenson, kept the lead line going constantly.

"Of all the nights I ever saw this is the worst," complained Harper. "The snow is coming down faster than ever and I'm afraid we're off course." At this moment the wheel refused to budge. "Here's worse luck still," he exclaimed, "the rudder chains are jammed."

"We are out of the channel, sir!" shouted Jorgenson from the deck. "She shoals again!—two fathoms, one, a half one fathom. We've hit the lower jetty, sir!" And the ship went crashing over the rotted timbers of the old submerged pier which had not felt a keel in over seventy years.

The Captain swore. His Presbyterian passenger seemed to concur silently. The tide was low and Harper's efforts to twist the *Wilmington* free only seemed to make matters worse. There was nothing to do but wait for high tide to float her clear.

All hands but Peter Jorgenson sought the comfort of the furnace fires. The mate walked the upper deck restlessly, immersed in the memories of the Christmas season in his own land. A sudden, icy gust of wind broke his reverie. As he turned in his pacing to and fro, he saw the dripping figure of a man leaning against the weather rail. The hair and beard were flecked with snow and the face was distorted with suffering.

"How did you get here? What do you want?" cried Peter, going forward with his hand outstretched to grasp the man. There was no answer. The figure raised a bony arm and pointed out over the water looking like some weird scarecrow of the deep.

"Who are you? Are you mad?" shouted Peter. As he reached out to lay hold of the figure his fingers met nothing but air. Where a man had stood a moment before there was now just the falling snow and darkness.

A few minutes later when Peter reached the pilot house his face was ashen with fear. The captain gave him an angry look and turning to McMillan said, "This man is drunk!"

"I am far from drunk," declared the mate. "I have not touched a drop. On my word, I have seen a ghost!"

"Now I know you're drunk!" exclaimed the Captain. "Who ever saw a ghost? McMillan, have you ever seen a ghost?"

"I do not doubt that Mr. Jorgenson has real reason for his alarm," replied McMillan. "I know of things in my experience beyond the realm of reason. But first let us search for Peter's ghost."

The captain agreed and the crew was called up and ordered to search the ship. McMillan joined the party and every corner was closely scrutinized by the light of the safety lamps. There was nothing to be found. Each man was questioned and all denied having seen anything out of the ordinary.

"The night is dark and perhaps you were having a dream," said the Captain to Jorgenson.

"Does a man having a dream walk in the bitter cold

with a lantern in his hand as I was doing then?" demanded Peter. "I stood within a yard of the stranger and I can never forget that fearful face. My lamp shown brightly and illuminated the figure clearly."

"Well, if ghosts are taking their walks tonight we may see troops of them before we get out of this confounded mess," said the Captain sarcastically. "How is the tide, Mr. Jorgenson?"

"It has been running up for quite two hours. She is already lifting a little, sir." In less than an hour more the steamer eased off the old jetty and was on her way again.

Suddenly, attracted by the wheel house lights, a blinded gull came crashing through the glass and fell dying at McMillan's feet.

"The foul fiend is certainly abroad tonight," cried the Scotsman, greatly shaken. "This is the worst of all bad omens."

But they had left the storm behind and the Captain was optimistic. Soon he began pointing out historic spots on the river shore as the lights of Kendal and Orton were safely passed.

"Eight years before the Boston Tea Party, of which so much is made, the minute men from Brunswick and Wilmington surrounded Tryon's Palace and demanded the surrender of the King's Commissioner. The Boston men disguised themselves as Indians. But Ashe and Waddell scorned such subterfuge and, seizing the British warship's rowing barge, they placed it on wheels and carried it in a triumphal march to Wilmington."

He had barely gotten these words out of his mouth when he and the others heard human cries.

"It is some poor castaway," said the Captain.

Reaching for the signal wire, he rang for a full stop. More desperate screams came from the water and brought McMillan from the wheel house with a look of terror on his face.

"On deck!" shouted the Captain.

"Aye, aye, sir!" came the answer from below.

Upon the troubled water, two cable lengths abeam, appeared a boat surrounded by a phosphorescent glow. It was an ancient rowing barge so foul with barnacles and slimy seaweed that Peter Jorgenson thought she must have been afloat a hundred years.

The Captain rubbed his eyes and looked again. "There's something uncanny about that thing. But it must be mortal men in trouble for spirits could not cry out with such anguish. Stand by and throw that barge a rope, Mr. Jorgenson."

The barge was soon just a cable length away. By now the horrified crew of the *Wilmington* beheld two gaunt human forms in tattered Highland dress from which emaciated legs emerged. Heavy chains extended from their ankles to their bloody wrists. As the barge with its grotesque occupants drew nearer McMillan saw their worn faces. Their hands were lifted beseechingly.

The Captain stood awe stricken at the sight. But suddenly, his voice trembling, he shouted to the mate, "Stand by and heave those men a line!"

Somehow, Peter made himself obey. At that moment the barge was lifted on a swelling wave which hurled it almost into his arms. Then as he heaved the rope across the rotten hulk, it and its shocking crew were gone!

The men of the *Wilmington* stood silent and appalled. Without a word the course was laid again.

But the ship had hardly resumed her speed when the sound of more shrieks came from the darkness just ahead. The ship was put out half speed as Peter shouted, "Starboard, hard a-starboard, sir; we are running down a wreck!"

The Captain wrenched the helm to one side, narrowly avoiding collision with what proved to be a vessel bottom up. Clinging to it were two exhausted seamen. The crew of the *Wilmington* helped the wretched men aboard.

As Peter held his lantern to the face of one of the seamen who had fainted on the deck, he cupped both hands around his mouth and shouted excitedly to the Captain.

"This is the man! This is the ghost I saw when we ran aground."

The skipper and McMillan studied the seaman's face intently. It was just as Jorgenson had described the face of the ghost—the vanishing stranger.

"How could this be?" exclaimed the Captain.

"His spirit was abroad in search of help," replied McMillan. "I've read and heard of similar phenomena."

"But how do you explain the phantom of the barge?"

"I dinna ken, I dinna ken," answered McMillan, lapsing into the Highland manner of speech. He would say no more.

After the castaways were fed they told their story. Their schooner, bound from Nassau for a northern port, had been wrecked by the gale off the coast. All the crew must have perished save these two men. They had clung fast to the hulk of their boat which had miraculously drifted into the river with the tide.

When asked if either of them had seen the *Wilming-*

ton before, the seaman whom Jorgenson recognized said he had been partly conscious for a time and thought he saw a steamer coming to their aid. But he could not for a moment recall the encounter described by the mate.

The Captain's eyes met those of McMillan, then turned away.

Swamp Girl

A SOUTH CAROLINA COUPLE PICKED UP A YOUNG GIRL WALKING BESIDE THE ROAD, ONLY TO RECEIVE THE SHOCK OF THEIR LIVES.

Between the gloomy depths of the dank South Carolina swamp and the moonlit ribbon of highway walked the solitary figure of a girl. She wore a black hat and a black suit and in her hand she carried a traveling bag.

On each side of the road beyond the shoulder was a steep drop of perhaps twenty feet to a drainage ditch. From the swamp's watery blackness rose the incessant rasping cheep of thousands of small creatures. Live oaks with their ragged gray shrouds of Spanish moss whispered among themselves with each passing breeze.

It was along this lonely stretch of highway, through the swamp toward Columbia, South Carolina, that the headlights of the car discovered her.

The driver of the car was a man whom we shall call J. C. Tipton. An employee of the Land Bank, he and his wife were on their way to Columbia. They wondered what a nicely dressed girl was doing walking alone along the highway at this late hour and slowed to stop to see if they could help her.

The girl thanked them. "Yes," she replied, "I am trying to get to Columbia to visit my mother, who is

113

desperately ill." She then gave them the address of a
house on Pickens Street. Since the car was a two door
sedan the man's wife courteously held the back of
her own seat to allow the girl to get in.

After the stranger was settled in the back, Mrs.
Tipton closed the car door and for a few minutes she

and her husband continued their conversation. Soon, however, Mrs. Tipton made a remark about the unseasonably hot weather, speaking over her shoulder to include the girl in the conversation. Hearing no answer she turned around to look in the back. Their passenger had vanished.

She peered down in the foot of the car but it, too, was empty. There was no possible way for anyone to get out of that car without the couple in the front seat knowing it.

Mrs. Tipton began to scream. Her husband, who was frightened too, almost ran off the road. Nothing he could say to his wife seemed to calm her. He was so concerned over her mounting hysteria that he drove to Columbia as quickly as possible and rushed his wife to a hospital. She was given sedatives to quiet her, and when the doctors told Tipton his wife

was resting comfortably and would be all right, he remembered the number on Pickens Street.

He decided he would go there and find out what he could. It was quite late when he finally reached the house. Although it was completely dark he decided he would ring the bell. He had waited several minutes before there was a flicker of light in the hall and a sleepy looking young man opened the door.

"You needn't tell me what you came for," the man said. "You came to tell me you picked up a young lady in the swamp and she disappeared."

Tipton was so surprised he couldn't say a word. He simply nodded.

"That was my sister," added the young man sadly. "She was killed in an automobile wreck in the swamp three years ago while she was on her way to the hospital to see our mother. Two other people have had the same experience you have, each time on the anniversary of her death."